THE SMASHING SCROLL

L D

~DRAWN

BY MICHAEL DAHL

ILLUSTRATED BY BRADFORD KENDALL

WITHDRAWN

Librarian Reviewer
Laurie K. Holland
Media Specialist

Reading Consultant
Elizabeth Stedem
Educator/Consultant

Raintree is an imprint of Capstone Global Library Limited, a
company incorporated in England and Wales having its registered
office at 7 Pilgrim Street, London, EC4V 6LB – Registered
company number: 6695582

"Raintree" is a registered trademark of Pearson Education
Limited, under licence to Capstone Global Library Limited

Text © Stone Arch Books, 2009
First published by Stone Arch Books in 2007
First published in hardback in the United Kingdom in 2009
First published in paperback in the United Kingdom in 2010
The moral rights of the proprietor have been asserted.

Art Director: Heather Kinseth
Cover Graphic Designer: Brann Garvey
Interior Graphic Designer: Kay Fraser
Edited in the UK by Laura Knowles
Printed and bound in China by Leo Paper Products Ltd

ISBN 978-1406212716 (hardback)
13 12 11 10 09
10 9 8 7 6 5 4 3 2 1

ISBN 978-1406212853 (paperback)
20 19 18 17 16 15
10 9 8 7 6 5 4

British Library Cataloguing in Publication Data
Dahl, Michael.
The smashing scroll. -- (Library of doom)
813.5'4-dc22
A full catalogue record for this book is available
from the British Library.

TABLE OF CONTENTS

 he Library of Doom is the world's largest collection of strange and dangerous books. The Librarian's duty is to keep the books from falling into the hands of those who would use them for evil purposes.

CHAPTER 1

SMASH!

At the edge of a giant city, a **dark wind** blows through the fields. The breeze slips through an open window.

Two young brothers sit in their room, reading comic books.

One of the comics is called *Smash*.

The younger brother found it **underneath** his bed that night.

As he reads, the pages **glow** with a strange light.

The young boy gets a strange look on his face.

The boy stands up and curls
his comic book into a tight roll.
He bangs it against his hand.

Smack!

"What are you doing?" asks
his brother.

Smack!

A loud noise comes crashing
through the window.

Smash!

The boy drops the comic book.

Both boys run to the window
to see what caused the crash.

The boys live on a farm with
barns and sheds and silos.

One of the **tall** stone silos has crashed to the ground.

It rolls across the ground like a huge rolling pin.

As the boys watch, the silo smashes into the barn and crushes it **flat.**

(CHAPTER 2)

THE SCROLL

High above the countryside, the Librarian is flying. He is searching for the lost books of **the Library of Doom.**

The Librarian hears something crash far below. The sound waves smash through the sky.

The Librarian is hit.

He is knocked out by the powerful sound waves. He falls towards the ground.

Down, down, he is falling into the path of the rolling stone silo.

The silo smashes over trees and fences. It smashes through houses.

As it rolls forwards, the silo leaves a trail of paper behind it.

The two boys see the Librarian's **dark shadow** hurtling down from the sky.

"He's falling towards that scroll," says the younger one.

"What do you mean, scroll?" asks his brother.

"I don't know," says the boy. "I just know that's what it is."

The Librarian's body is falling directly **in front** of the moving scroll.

Suddenly, he **stops.** The Librarian floats gently above the moving scroll.

The Librarian wakes up, still floating. Below him he sees letters written on a giant roll of paper. "The Scroll!" he says to himself.

CHAPTER 3

THE LAST STORY

The giant silo is really a scroll. As it smashes through the countryside, it unrolls its **magic page.**

People out walking at night are trapped by the giant covering of the scroll's page.

The two young boys can see where the scroll's page begins. It started when the scroll **smashed** through their barn.

"Look!" says the older brother. "It's a bunch of words."

"What is this all about?" asks the father.

"It's a story," says the younger brother.

The boys and their father read the words written at the top of the scroll's page. *The World's Last Story,* it says.

"How can it be the last story?"
asks the older brother.

The Librarian still **floats** above the scroll's page.

He quickly reads the story. Now he understands the scroll's evil magic.

The scroll's story was written by a powerful wizard called the **Spellbinder**.

The Spellbinder was waiting for a person to read a special comic near the hidden scroll.

Then the scroll would **unwind** its magic page.

On and on the scroll would smash until the **whole world** was covered by its unrolling paper.

CHAPTER 4

THE
CHASE!

The Librarian spreads his arms wide and rushes through the air.

Far ahead, the scroll is smashing cars parked along a lonely street.

Crunch! Smash!

A car is **turning a corner**. Inside are a group of friends coming from a birthday party.

The driver of the car sees something strange in her mirror.

"What's that?" she yells.

Her friends look through the rear window and see the scroll. One of them **screams**.

"Hurry!" shouts her friend. "Go faster!"

The young woman pushes on the accelerator. The car **speeds** down the road.

"It's still coming!" yells a friend.

The scroll is moving faster, too.
Soon it will **crash** over the car.

The Librarian appears above the car. His boots **crunch** on the car's roof as he stands to face the scroll.

He reaches into his coat and pulls out a `small` book.

It reads *The World's First Story*.

The Librarian **throws** the book at the bottom of the scroll.

The book hits the bottom of the scroll. The scroll bounces up. It flies higher and higher. Its shadow passes across the moon, and then disappears.

The car squeals to a stop. The friends **pour** out of the doors.

"What happened?" they ask. "Where did that thing go?"

The driver looks at the roof of her car. She sees two prints where boots once stood. Then she looks up and sees a `shadow` pass across the moon.

~ꙮ THE END ꙮ~

A PAGE FROM THE LIBRARY OF DOOM

SCROLLS

A scroll is a piece of paper or parchment with writing on it, rolled up into a tube. Some scrolls are attached to a wooden rod or baton at either end. A scroll is read by unrolling the paper.

Scrolls can be read top to bottom, right to left, or left to right.

In Jewish synagogues, places of worship, the holy writings known as the Torah, are written on a scroll. Someone reads from the scroll during the worship service.

In China, artists paint on scrolls made of parchment and silk. The art of scroll painting is at least 4,000 years old!

In films and television programmes, the credits continually move across the screen. Viewers read the credits as if they were reading from an unrolling scroll. Now when writing moves across a screen, it is called *scrolling*.

ABOUT THE AUTHOR

Michael Dahl is the author of more than 100 books for children and young adults. He has twice won the AEP Distinguished Achievement Award for his non-fiction. His Finnegan Zwake mystery series was chosen by the Agatha Awards to be among the five best mystery books for children in 2002 and 2003. He collects books on poison and graveyards, and lives in a haunted house in Minneapolis, USA.

ABOUT THE ILLUSTRATOR

Bradford Kendall has enjoyed drawing for as long as he can remember. As a boy, he loved to read comic books and watch old monster films. He graduated from the Rhode Island School of Design with a BFA in Illustration. He has owned his own commercial art business since 1983, and lives in Providence, Rhode Island, USA, with his wife, Leigh, and their two children Lily and Stephen. They also have a cat named Hansel and a dog named Gretel. Sometimes, they all sit together to watch an old monster film.

GLOSSARY

accelerator (ak-SEL-er-ay-ter) – pedal that controls the speed of a car

hurtling (HUR-tuhl-ing) – falling or moving quickly

rolling pin (ROH-ling pin) – a long, round wooden tube used in baking for flattening dough

scroll (SKROHL) – a sheet of paper with writing on it wrapped into a tube shape

silo (SY-loh) – a tall, round building used for storing grain

spellbinder (SPEL-byn-dur) – a person who puts a spell on another person or object

DISCUSSION QUESTIONS

1. Why do you think the Spellbinder used someone reading a comic book to start the smashing scroll?

2. Why do you think the Librarian was flying over the countryside? Do you think he knew something evil was about to happen? Explain.

3. The story on the giant scroll was called *The World's Last Story*. Why do you think it was called that? Who do you think wrote that story on the scroll?

WRITING PROMPTS

1. Imagine that you live on a farm next to the boys' farm. You wake up and see the giant scroll smashing through the countryside. Does it come near your house? What does it sound like? Describe what happens to you that night.

2. The Spellbinder is never shown in the story. Read carefully about the wizard (on pages 21 and 22) and you'll see we don't know if it is a man or a woman. What do you think the Spellbinder looks like? Write a description.

MORE BOOKS TO READ

This story may be over, but there are many more dangerous adventures in store for the Librarian. Will the Librarian be able to escape the cave of the deadly giant bookworms? Will he defeat the rampaging Word Eater in time to save the world? You can only find out by reading the other books from the Library of Doom...